In memory of Robert Francis Iacarella, my brother. His love of marine life: scuba diving, fishing and boating, was a dream realized in his life, as he shared this with his beloved son, Lucas Robert Iacarella.

Dedication to: my husband Kelly, my children: Jeremiah (Katie), Jennifer, Joseph, Veronica (Marcus), Luke (Michala).
My grandchildren: Max, Avalon, Austin, Alexandra, and Troy.
To my extended family and friends.

Credit to: Jennifer, my daughter, for her love, inspiration, and passion for wildlife, which inspired me to write this book.

Credit to: Luke, my son, for his technical skill in comprising this book for publication.

Credit to: Jennifer Soriano, who enhanced the original artwork with her quilling talent.

"Finny, the Lonesome Dolphin" is a children's storybook about a dolphin that becomes separated from his family after playing a game of "Hide and Seek." Through a series of adventures and setbacks, he embarks on a lonely journey of trying to find his family, while learning about the world all around him and about himself. He has close encounters of the oceanic kind, both friendly and dangerous, while the sun is his guide to light the way for his family reunion in the end.

Children learn about dolphins, sea creatures and the challenges o life in the ocean. It also emphasizes the importance of the role of family support for happiness and survival. It sheds light on the importance of faith in life, in the example of the "sun" giving its warmth and light for guidance and protection.

The artwork is colorful and vibrant in movement and expression, enhanced through the unique use of quilling. It is designed to aid children in their reading, imagination, and learning skills. This storybook was well received by elementary school children.

In the wavy waters
of the deep blue sea,
lives a friendly dolphin,
whose name is "Finny."
He is one of the fastest
swimmers in the sea!
He loves to frolic and play
games with his family!

One day, while at play,
in a game of "Hide and Seek,"
Finny was the one busy counting,
while his family was busy hiding.
He had promised not to peek!

While Finny took his time counting
out loud,
"One...two...three...four...five...six...
seven...eight...nine...ten..."
he did not know that an undertow
had pulled him further out to sea,
and far, far away from his family

When Finny stopped counting,
he opened his eyes and shouted,
"Ready or not, here I come!"
Finny swam up...He swam down...He
swam all around...
His dolphin family was nowhere nee
to be found!
Instead, he found himself, very los
and lonesome!

After a very long and lonely time, much to his surprise, a cheery bright-red sailboat passed right before his eyes!

Finny raced to catch up to it,
to see if it would like to play;
but the sailboat, being pushed by
the wind,
could not stop to play with him!
Finny watched in sad dismay, as th
sailboat sailed away...
Out of sight and out of the bay!

Then Finny saw something he had
never seen before!
It was a floating buoy, not far from
the shore!
Finny swam underneath it, pushing
with his nose!
It just sat still in the very same place
and in the very same pose!

While basking in the sun's rays,
Finny felt so light-hearted, dancing
upon the waves!
He was having fun
with the sun! From there,
a special friendship had begun!

The sun was smiling at Finny!
The dolphin did a flip in the air!
Finny was so happy to have this
great friend, one who would
always be there!!

Later that day,
Finny dove far down into the
deep, with his heart still
set on finding his family and
making friends to keep!

Finny swam near a jellyfish,
hoping it would play;
but it took one look at Finny and
quickly swam away!
Next, he startled an octopus
nearby. It took off so fast, Finny
had no chance to say hi or
goodbye!

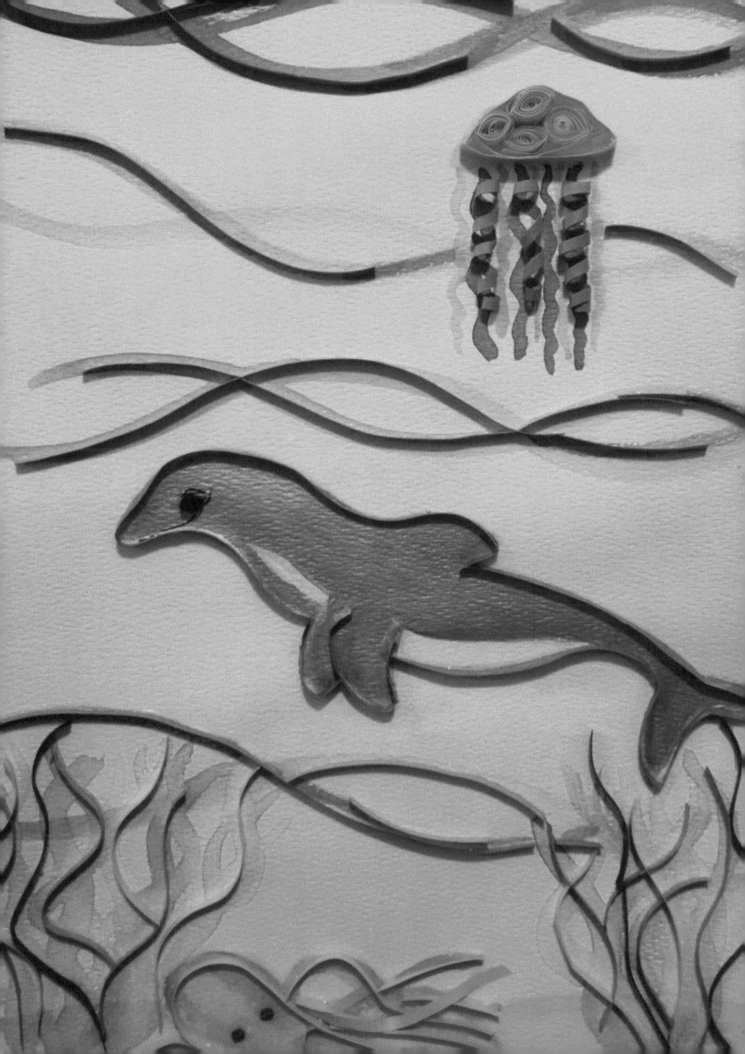

Then suddenly, out of the dark, came a big hungry shark on the hunt for another meal!

Finny swam fast and far away to safety!

He left that big, hungry shark reeling with his stomach still empty!

Finny was in for another scare, when he came across a diving blue whale!! Finny swam for his life, when he was almost hit by the blue's gigantic tail!!!

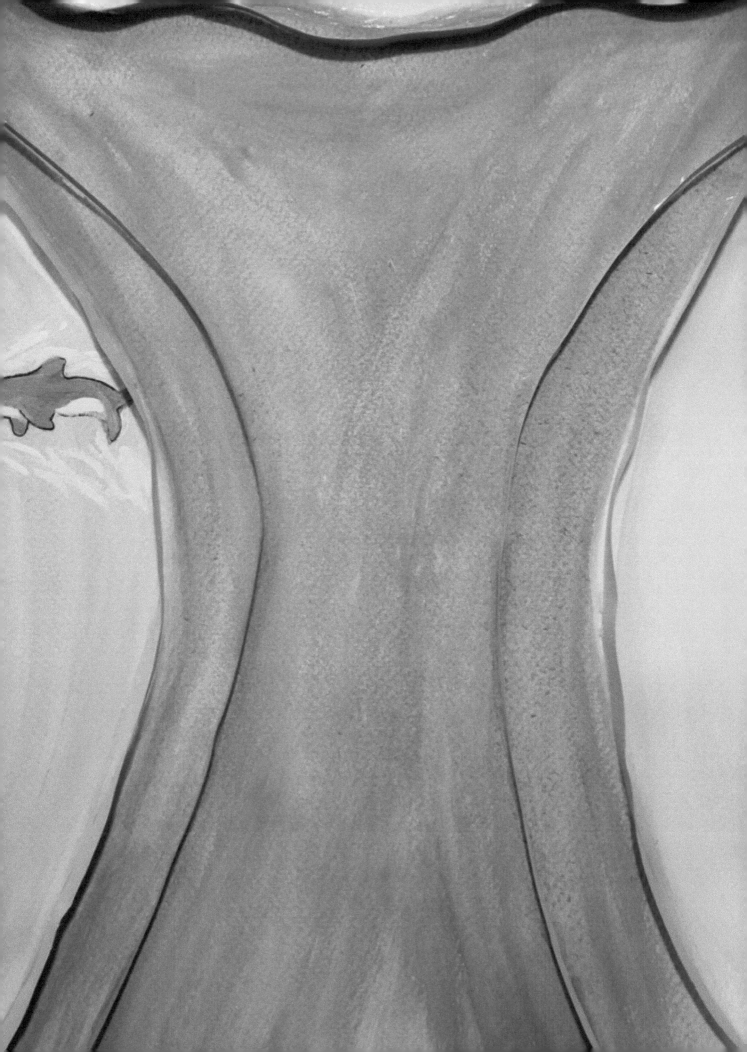

Sometime later, Finny noticed that
big sea turtle was gracefully
swimming by,
when something else, most unusual
had suddenly caught his eye!
It was a deep-sea diver exploring th
coral reef!
Finny found him to be quite friendl
much to his relief!

Finny towed him around
by his dorsal fin.
He was so happy
the diver would play with him!
They had so much fun together,
Finny wanted it to last forever!
He felt sad when
their playtime had to end,
but he would always remember him
as a very good friend!

While swimming through
the deep blue sea,
Finny was amazed to see,
so many fish of every size, shape,
and color!
It made Finny sad to think that
though there were so many,
not a single one of them was his
friend, sister, or brother!

"Where, oh where is my family?"
Finny wondered.
"Where, oh where could they be?"
Finny felt so very sad and lonesome
that he began to weep.
Then ever so gently came familiar
sounds echoing from the deep!
The moment they had reached his ear
it made his dolphin heart leap!

Overjoyed, Finny exclaimed, "My family, could it really be?"
He could hardly believe it!
Quick as a flash, Finny raced toward the sounds to get a close look.
Then he cried out from his heart in sound all his own, and that was all i took!

Upon hearing him, up out of the blue, came his long-lost, now-found family! "Finny!!! Hooray!!!" They all cheered, leaping around him so happily!

The sun was so delighted
to see them reunited,
as Finny, with his family,
swam back to their home
in the sea!
Together, they would always be,
as one big happy family!

The end!

CPSIA information can be obtained
at www.ICGtesting.com
Printed in the USA
BVHW021042220621
610209BV00002B/82